M-BRANE SF PRESENTS

THE 12 BURNING WHEELS

BY CESAR TORRES

The 12 Burning Wheels © 2010
by Cesar Torres
www.cesartorres.net

Published by *M-Brane SF*
www.mbranesf.blogspot.com
Cover photography by Farhan Bokhari
Cover design by Cesar Torres
Title font is "Yellow Magician" by
Erico Lebedenco
www.ericolebedenco.com

The publisher thanks
D.D. Tannenbaum for his
generous assistance in programming
ebook editions for Kindle and Mobipocket

**M-Brane SF is a proud member
of the Outer Alliance.
This is our Mission Statement:**

*"As a member of the Outer Alliance, I advocate
for queer speculative fiction and those who
create, publish and support it, whatever their
sexual orientation and gender identity. I
make sure this is reflected in my actions
and my work."*
www.outeralliance.org

*Dedicated to
my family.*

FOREWORD

The fact that you hold this book in your hands (or view it on your screen) is partially the result of a happy social media accident. One morning on Twitter, book publicist and good pal Matt Staggs recommended that I follow one of his Twitter friends, a guy using the charming handle "Urraca." Matt doesn't give bad advice, so I immediately started following this Urraca, who turned out to be Cesar Torres. Curious to know more about my new friend, I checked out his blog, and soon we were chatting on Twitter. He showed me a lovely short story called "Mantis Love," which you are about to read in this collection, and told me that it is one of twelve stories that he wrote in twelve days as part of a creative challenge to himself.

I was immediately taken with the idea of bringing these twelve stories to the world under one cover. And this was after having read *only* "Mantis Love" and one other unrelated story, but none of the other eleven "wheels." But at the time, I was busy putting together *Things We Are Not*, my recent anthology of queer science fiction, and I didn't have room for a new project. Also, I think of ideas for books constantly and abandon most of them as either impractical or simply not as great as I thought they were when they first crossed my mind. But the idea that the world might need *this* book from Cesar Torres kept haunting me, and I asked him eventually to show me rest of the stories. I read them all in one session and decided about a minute later that I'd be a fool to not do whatever I can to bring Cesar's singular vision to the attention of as many readers as possible.

The result is before you now, dear reader, *The 12 Burning Wheels* complete, and you are in for some serious pleasure whether you take these stories in little doses, one at a time, or read them all in a single sitting. Each of Cesar's twelve tales is a unique thing. No two of them are quite alike, yet together they create a single impression of a world radiant with an aura of mystery and magic, a land full of the bizarre and the dangerous and the beautiful, a shimmering region of horror, wonder and love. This may be your first visit to his world, but I am sure it will not be your last.

—Christopher Fletcher, *M-Brane SF*

1

THE BROKEN
CHEST

Without a sliver of a doubt, the Sphinxe was the best aura technologist of his time. He'd rather be called a magician, but he gave up on that antiquated title at the age of fifty-six, when *People* magazine listed him as one of the one hundred sexiest people alive. His lantern jaw, the hint of stubble, the deep-set black eyes, he saw them as nothing more than skin and bone.

To a nation of millions, the Sphinxe was a celebrity, a man of science and dark matter, a master of the creatures that science still could not explain. He didn't care for the talk shows, or the awards. He only cared for his wife, Alicia, and his daughter, Iphigenia.

On Iphigenia's eighth birthday, the Sphinxe presented her with a smoky blue glass leaf, light as, flexible and fragile, but transparent as river water. "Where does it come from?" she asked, rubbing her left eye, as she did when presented with objects that piqued her interest. Using a mechanical pencil, the Sphinxe drew for her a sketch of a delicate-looking plant in a jungle clearing. "It's a leaf from the Broken Chest plant," he said. "I made this plant for you."

He had made the plant, he explained, from three thousand eagle tears and the livers of three dozen human cadavers. The plant, its stalk and leaves fashioned from pink and black human skin, lived in a secret location in the jungles of Merida, Mexico, its silver roots dug three hundred feet into the earth. The Sphinxe explained to his daughter that he had planted the Broken Chest a mile down the road from where his mother and father lay buried in a cemetery.

Iphigenia tucked the leaf into her hair and ran off to her bedroom.

The day after, at breakfast, the Sphinxe asked Iphigenia where she had put the leaf. "I ate it," she said.

During the day, as Iphigenia opened birthday presents and petted her new seven-headed hydra, the sun rose, yellow as yolk, but the sky did not light up in blue as it had done for millions of years before. Instead, its wide expanse glowed deep green, the color of moss. While the journalists came to the Sphinxe's home to ask him questions about the event, military task forces scoured the Pyrenees, the bottom of the Red Sea and even the

Himalayas in search of the source of the green sky. Scientists and aura engineers set to work to figure out how the sky could tint itself like a chameleon does. After a few decades, they gave up.

The sky remained green for the rest of Iphigenia's lifetime, which extended far beyond that of her father, who, at the age of seventy-three, collapsed one morning from heart failure as he made his way down to the cellar. After his funeral, Iphigenia said goodbye to her twelve-year-old son and flew to Merida, where she walked the jungle, alone. Her feet made soft padding sounds on the wet ground. The spiders and jaguars she met along the way shone with an emerald sheen, and they watched her in silence. She walked as far into the jungle as her middle-aged legs could carry her, then sat in a clearing to rest and drink water from her canteen.

Through the crooked shadows of the cast by the midday sun, she spotted a light object, curled and soft. She walked toward it, bending over to see it up close. It was an odd plant, colored vanilla and chocolate along its trunk and sporting crystalline, transparent leaves that hung low over the ground like watery limbs. It whispered to her, though what it was trying to say she would never know.

Without thinking twice, Iphigenia plucked one of its leaves and ate it. She knew even as she put it to her lips that this was the Broken Chest plant. She chewed with relish, smiling as her teeth ground down on the fibrous pulp. Then, without warning, the light around her began to change, as if there were an eclipse.

Iphigenia looked up. The sky pulsed like a beating heart and wove itself into a purple fabric, deep as night. The sun shone like a yellow button on plum felt. Birds screamed in surprise, and monkeys howled. She paused for a moment, then she ate another leaf, and the sky beat faster, turning red as blood, the clouds a clam pink.

She put another leaf in her mouth and chewed. She cherished its sweet, pulpy taste of mint. The sky filled with light as it returned to blue, the color it had been when Iphigenia was a child.

Memories fluttered toward her then, like brusque birds and velvet moths. She remembered her father, his ill temper and his generous spirit, who tried teaching her aura engineering principles but failed. She remembered his coughing fits from too many cigars and the soft pecks he laid on her mother's forehead after arguments about money.

She remembered her father's diplomas and the awards he received for the tools he developed to harness magic and subatomic particles. She remembered the firm words of inspiration he said to her every day and the way his anger crackled when he lost his patience. She remembered his face, weathered like speckled leather, creased at the mouth, soft smile in the wings.

Iphigenia looked up at the blue sky again and felt a pang of relief to see it shine once more, like an upside-down pool of water. She plucked another crystalline leaf from the Broken Chest, and when she did so, she heard it squeal, like a strained violin string.

She placed the leaf in her pocket. Her youngest son would turn seven that day, and she wanted to make it back to California in time to give him his birthday present. She hoped for a yellow sky, but its new hue would belong to her son, and only to her son.

2

THE SCRYER

If I wasn't in such a hurry, I'd take my time choosing the right tool, but when I look down at my watch I notice it's almost nine. The store is going to close, and I need a scryer. Like, now. I look out the window of the shop, and Lake Street looks deserted. Good. The dudes that started following me might have lost me when I turned the corner onto Halsted Street, but I can't take chances.

Jesus, I've never sweated this hard. My T-shirt is soaked.

I need a scryer, and quick. I could use a Big Gulp, too, but first things first.

The scryers are under a glass counter in one neat row. Of course, the mirrored kind are always a good choice. The obvious choice, classic models. Most are shaped like bowls, half moons of knowledge. I peer into their concave surfaces and see my face reflected upside down, twisted like taffy, and my gut rubs along the surface of the counter, squeaking. I should go on a diet, I tell myself, as I see my pear shape in the scryers below. I hate my reflection. The smallest mirror bowl is the size of a dinner plate. If those guys are really following me, I can't carry something that big. It won't do.

I can feel my skin begin to crawl with gooseflesh and a wave of electricity comes over me, like the first time on a rollercoaster. I'm 27 years old, I just lost my virginity an hour ago, and in the process, I killed the girl.

I never meant to do it. Who does? It was an accident. I'm not even sure how it happened. The tangle of white sheets and her creamy skin swirl like a vortex in my mind and I find myself missing her already. So much whiteness, so much of it. Even my semen came out wet and white, and I laid panting, wondering why the first time felt so scary. I wasn't her first, I was sure of it, and that was fine. She knew the right places to work, the right positions, the way to pleasure me.

Shitty hotel along Halsted, fleabag and junkie heaven. We lay together, folded on top of one another like eaves on a roof. The whiskey still pumped fumes up through my throat and I felt sick bed spins coming on, but, fuck, I had just made love. To a woman.

I blinked in the dim fluorescent light, and next thing I knew she was twitching. Not twitching like a nervous tick, but twitching like a tuning fork, her eyes rolled in the back of her head like wet marbles. Her mouth flew open and she stopped breathing, I could tell. Did she have some condition? A heart attack? Stroke?

So quiet. I patted her cheek to wake her up, to get her breathing again, but instead her mouth spilled black stuff all over the white sheets and her fair skin. I fought the urge to vomit and knew it was time to get the hell out of there. The stuff moved on its own, crawling off her mouth and up my arm, getting into my hair.

If I left the hotel room quickly, no one would find out I was ever there. Fuck if I was going to call an ambulance. As far as I'm concerned, this was *her* fault. She should have told me she had some disease. Bitch. Even as I yanked my clothes back on I realized the black stuff was a mass of black worms, like black maggots but worse. They bit my arms, but by the time I bled, I was already running down the street.

It was when I was three blocks away from the hotel that I realized a group of men was following me. They moved like shadows along the street, but that's what any guy looks like walking at night in the city, you know? I picked up my pace, and when I got to Halsted, I bolted straight into the pawnshop.

And so here I am, greased up like a pig

from all the sex sweat an hour before and trying to just get the fuck over losing my cherry to a dead girl.

I'm far too old to be a virgin. But programmers like me don't get girls often, and when we do we have to go and get it. This was my chance. Now I'm fucked.

At the end of the glass counter, after all the large font-shaped bowls and mirrors, lies a single scryer, orange as a tangerine, shaped like a Swiss Army Knife. I hand over three 20s to the clerk and I get the hell out of the store. Fuck the change and I don't have time to read the instruction packet.

I head toward the closest L station and I blow dust off the surface of the scryer. Its glossy surface is hard to read but it sits in my palm with a comfortable weight. I can see my round face turned into an opal in its convex surface. It's got a furry tip and a crease on its underside. It's the oddest fucking scryer I've ever seen.

I sit in the last car of the train, which is now headed for the Loop. Three men sit in the front, their backs turned to me, and in between, only grimy windows and bacteria-covered seats separate us. I gaze into the mirrorlike surface of the orange oblong and I begin to scry.

Most scryers only show you about a few hours' worth of the past, which is about all I need. In the scryer's surface I see the taxi door open as she meets me at happy hour, how happy she is to have pulled her hair back and to be wearing a summer dress. It's so vivid I can almost smell her deodorant and the sweetness between her legs.

The scryer flickers and I am moved forward, to the table where we're doing our fifth whiskey shot. I've got my hand running down her leg. She tells me she's good at it, and I giggle to myself. This will be better than all the Asian girls in porn flicks. I wonder then if she considers going down on a guy as second or third base.

The scryer flickers one more time and time has moved forward again. I see the hotel bed where we're making love as if I am taping it from above with a camera. We're grinding in the sheets. My hairy back obscures her tiny body, but I feel aroused regardless. Of course, what I don't see is that she's dying on me even as she is reaching orgasm, and I can't figure out why. She's dead by the time I come, though I was in such a daze when it happened in real time that I stopped paying attention to her. Then there are black worms licking the sweat off her breasts and burying themselves in my armpit hair as I try to get out of there. She's dead, and I have no answers.

I put the scryer in my other hand and I grunt. It reminds me of a butterfly cocoon. Unusual, but it has no answers. A waste of sixty dollars. Fuck. Why did she die?

Then the scryer does something different. Its surface begins to glow orange, like a fiery eye. The reflection on its shell takes me back, much further back than a day, back hundreds of years in fact. I am not sure how I know I am going so far back in time, but I can tell we are on the American continent; I can see buffalo in the distance and an eagle flying overhead. I know to my right there's a village nearby, and the Europeans have not yet arrived to colonize, but it doesn't matter. The scryer wants me to see the round hill in front of me, where something's stirring and coming up to breathe.

The scryer wants me to see the female body emerging from the ground, being born as a full adult with sensual hips and full breasts with small nipples and skin white as bone. Her hair is white and I can see her moist tongue is the color of milk. Black particles cling to her as she emerges in the dusk, and my heart sinks as I begin to recognize her face. It's the chick I just slept with, the one that shook to death on me. She's a Worm Queen, and I know so because every single orifice on her body is sprouting black worms. She bleeds in black, licking her lips as the black maggots sip at the salt in her tear ducts.

Why didn't I realize she was a Worm Queen before? The scryer tells me this is the shy girl I met at the company party last month, the one I asked out, knowing she'd be shy and somewhat naive. She knew I thought she might be an easy lay, but she did not know then that she would be my first.

I think about how I humiliated her body just an hour ago, and, as the train rumbles on the tracks, I feel a touch of remorse that slowly begins to turn into something else: victory. Damn. I have just fucked and killed a Worm Queen. Who else can lay claim to that? As far as I know, Worm Queens went extinct in the past fifty years. Biology 101. But the scryers are never wrong. This is a Worm Queen. Or was. I begin to get hard again at the excitement of it.

The guys at the office won't believe me, but I've got the orange scryer and I can show them. I can even brag about this scryer, which goes way back further than a day. Fuck yeah. I fucked a Worm Queen to death. The only thing that will come after such a victory will be more ass for me. My time as a pussyless virgin has ended, my friends.

I look up, and I can see we're right about to enter the Loop, and I'm thinking I can go get something to eat to soak up all the booze, get myself home, shower, maybe think about how to celebrate. It's not too late. I could use some of this raw energy and hook up with another girl. Why not?

The three guys at the front of the L car must have switched seats or something, because now they are in the middle of the car, and why is the train taking so long? It's as if we're forever riding the rails but never reaching our stop. The lights flicker above, and the guys stare at me, hunched within their black trench coats. Their faces are identical, like triplets', black hair and brown eyes. They smile, and one of them croaks, the way a swamp animal might in the middle of the night. They smile again, and I look down at my scryer. One of the men puts his fingers up to his face as if he has a scryer himself. Fucking homeless, I think. Whatever.

I follow his lead, hold the scryer up to my face and I scry. I can see the image on the surface of the scryer while keeping an eye on the three guys in coats, and the scryer takes me back in the past again, at least in my right eye.

I'm in a dusty field, and I can see in the distance the Chicago skyline. It's not the complete skyline, though; it must be the early twentieth century. I can see three young boys playing with their sister, an older sister who seems far too adult, too womanly to have such young siblings, with skin white as a cloud and black stains on her lips. The four of them giggle together.

My left eye brings me back to the three guys in the car with me. I know right there and then these are her three brothers. The scryer doesn't need to tell me that.

But there's no male equivalent of

Worm Queens, I remind myself. Everyone learns that in school. They breed in eggs, like insects, without insemination from males. There are only female Worm Queens. Or were, motherfucker! Heh, heh. I did the last Worm Queen, I remind myself. My right eye returns to the image in the orange scryer.

Her three brothers move long locks of straight black hair away from their brows and pick the black worms out of her hair. One of them plucks a black speck from her shoulder with his index finger and thumb, and he pops it in his mouth. They eat the worms with relish.

How in the hell can she have brothers? It doesn't matter I tell myself. I put the scryer in my pocket and replay the sweet smile on her lips as she went down on me, sexual pleasure flooding my blood, my head and the sheets. So much whiteness. And to think I killed what was possibly the last Worm Queen. A smile plays on my lips.

The three men in coats, shoulders hunched, are now seated right in front of me and I notice they are smiling just like me. They push locks of hair from their brows, and the black hair flops back over their foreheads. Their teeth shimmer like moonlight in the dim lights of the train car. I clutch the scryer, but I realize they don't want my scryer, or my money. They only want their sister back.

Any question I might have had about

their nature is quickly resolved. They're definitely not like their sister. My heart sinks. They groan and their bones crack like twigs. They have probably fed off their sister for decades, cleaning her of the worms that spilled from her, but now their sister is dead. They look hungry.

They rise, popping and bending, elongating and shifting, the height of men, but they are no longer men. They are three black birds with razor sharp black beaks, and their onyx eyes blink in unison as they spread their wings backward through the rumbling train car. Giant birds, black as night, monstrous ravens.

I put my hands in front of my face just as they lunge at me. They pluck at my chest and at my genitals, and my flesh tears. They pick at the scryer from the torn hole in my trousers and I see one of them has my tongue in its carbon beak. They devour their feast with a hunger worse than my own. They will finish me in seconds, and the last thing I can see is my slipping muscle and the tendons of my face reflected in the scryer shaped like an orange cocoon.

3

HONEY

When three days pass, all you will need will be honey. The transformation will only take three days. It's been that way since I have existed.

On the first night, you will wake up in your bed, or maybe in the woods. We never know how this might happen.

You will look around you, and you will notice you are mostly naked, though clothed by the garment of wolf fur that protects your loins.

You will not be cold. You will not feel warm, either. Things will be just right.

You will awake, and light will flood your surroundings. These surroundings can be the city, or the woods. Nowadays, there are various places you may awaken.

You will love your bone and sinew, your cartilage and its web of fascia.

On the second night, you will think about how connected you are to me, the female, the one that governs over your soul, or what's left of it.

You will awaken bathed in light, white as chalk, never yellow.

You will be brethren to the snake, cousin to the boar, a distant relative of the owl. But when you open your eyes in this wonderful white light, you will recognize them by their true names, and you will see the memories of blood on their fangs, their snouts and their carnivorous beaks. They will try to lead you astray occasionally with their false tales of sorcery and witch's curses, but pay no mind to them. Do not take pity, do not dab at their tears. You will only recall whispers.

You will remember into the future, and you will forecast the past. In these halls of remembrance lost and omen buried, you might hear some of the names they call me. None of these names is true. What is true is the white warmth of my light that bathes you when you awaken.

You will awake, of course, at night.

On the third night, you will have a hunger in your heart and deep in your belly. You will kill to satiate yourself with flesh and think of me often.

The men, the ordinary men, they will have a name for you. They might even hunt you. You may tear at them and eat their arms, their faces and their penises, if you so wish.

Of course, every time you awake, naked, in the belt of fur, scratching at the hair on your chest and your smooth arms, you will taste the metallic feast of blood.

On this third night you will eat of the flower in the forest, you will be bitten by a wasp. Do not fear the wasp. She is mine, too.

Sometimes she will whisper one of my old names, Circe. The name itself will sound like a whisper. I do not mind. I no longer breathe.

When the wasp stings you, she will lead you to her nest. This will happen in the blackest of night. And you shall put your mouth, or your beast jaw — your choice — at the tip of the hive. You will be stung thousands of times by wasps, but your tongue, bloated and poisoned, will probe the hive well. Inside, you will find the sweetest nectar. Honey that will taste as good as the flesh and guts of the deer you seek at night. It will taste better than virgin blood. It will remind you of me. The honey on your tongue will linger forever. And then you will return, on the verge of death, to your sleeping place and begin anew.

On the fourth night, you will be officially mine, part of my legion, my army. And you will help me devour the men, the undeserving ones and the righteous ones. You will help me eat humanity. You will serve me, whether you are a man in a belt of black fur or a wolf, large as a mare with teeth sharp as blades. You will help me eat the men of the world.

You will consume with me, and within me. And you will know the taste of honey and blood, and the taste of the white light of the moon, and you will savor the dusty creak of old memories. The gutted flesh in front of you will generate curling ribbons of steam in the woods and in the city, and you shall devour before it turns cold and stiff.

You will love me.

4

MANTIS LOVE

SMS transcript, May 2005.

Ned: *My mom says I can go to prom with you. I gots permission!*

Martin: *Love it*

Ned: *But we can't crash at a hotel that night. She won't allow it.*

Martin: *Why not? It's not like anyone's going to get pregnant.*

Ned: *Says too young*

Martin: *Come on! We're seniors.*

Ned: *Whatev. Can't. We can make out, though. You know, mess around.*

Martin: *Not. Good. Enough.*

Ned: *I want 2 too*

Martin: *I know*

Ned: *I can bring my Mantis.*

Martin: *Why?*

Ned: *Buncha seniors are riding in on unicycles. Why shouldn't I?*

Martin: *OK*

Ned: *For fun. Somethin different.*

Martin: *Those things don't work. My dad calls them carny junk. You have one?*

Ned: *Yup*

Martin: *Bunk*

Ned: *They work, it's true. My grandpa says they're like magnets for all sorts of things. Weird things.*

Martin: *Huh?*

Ned: *Creatures. Whatever. I can ride it tho. You should see me. I'll teach you. I can teach you things.*

Martin: *I just want you to teach me what your sweet spot is.*

Ned: *You're crazy*

Martin: *XOXOXOX*

From Martin's Journal, June 2005

Ned did show up to prom on his Mantis after all. He told me to wait for him at the front door while all the bros went around me like I was the living dead. After about twenty minutes, I saw him come around the corner.

Wow. I had never seen a Mantis before, just in books. It had scuffs all along the seat and on its red metal paint. But Len didn't care. He rode the thing into the prom, right past me and through the doors, and I've never heard so much applause.

I wasn't sure where to stand, and the crowd shoved me out of the way as he made his way to the center. He rode in circles for a few minutes, never losing his balance. It was awesome. Then someone behind me yelled *"Faggot."*

Whatever. They say that word all the time in the halls, in the locker room, at the bus stop. Nothing new.

Other kids came into the gym on unicycles, but no one dared do it on a Mantis. Len was the only one who could ride it. While the unicycles put their riders at a height of about six feet, Mantis put him about nine feet in the air. He was the skinniest giant on a single wheel that I've ever seen. I wanted to kiss him already.

And then someone knocked Ned off

the thing. He fell like he was stage-diving at a rock show. Someone else threw a paper cup full of soda at his head. And someone else stepped on the wheel of the Mantis, bending its spokes. There was more faggot this, faggot that, and the hets who were with us began to shove back and forth. The rented tuxes and pastel dresses became a tangle. I wasn't sure who was with us and who wasn't. I tasted blood from where someone punched me in mouth, but it didn't matter 'cause it felt good for me to kick him back in the nuts.

Somewhere along the way I felt a hot bud of fire on my face, and when I looked down, there was a flap of my cheek hanging off it. Small cut, but the bruise swelled up like a gory plum. My ribs hurt.

And then the cops were already on their way. They pulled us apart, the adults did. Someone spit at Ned, but I never saw who it was.

The newspaper lady showed up, and the dudes from the TV station were there, too. They called me and Ned brave.

Whatever. I was so bored already.

The best part is that Ned's parents came to pick us up. I just wanted to go home. Prom just sucks. I knew it was going to suck from the moment I had to rent that cheap-looking tux. They dropped me off at home, and it was all sorts of weird giving Ned a goodbye kiss in front of his mom, so we didn't.

The next day I walked over to Ned's

house. His Mantis lay in two pieces on the driveway. Just a wheel and, about a foot away, a little scuffed-up seat. Someone had scrawled "Faggot" in chalk on the sidewalk. I rubbed my foot over the letters and they blurred a bit.

"My parents are at the groceries," Ned said. We each carried a piece of the Mantis and put them in his garage. "It's virtually dead," he said. "Whatever tricks the Mantis had in it, they're gone. My grandpa's going to have a heart attack. He had only lent it to me."

Before Ned could rattle on some more, I leaned over the hood of his mom's car and I kissed him. Just had to. Ned's a good kisser, and I could feel the hardness of his shoulders through his Aphex Twin T-shirt. He tasted like something in a medicine cabinet, sweet, like Pepto-Bismol. I liked the bits of stubble on his chin. I was so happy. As we dug around on top of each other in the humid garage, the two halves of the Mantis squealed like rusty hinges under my foot. I must have stepped on them. Crunch. There goes that spoke.

And then I heard the screech.

The pieces of metal and the rubber wheel squealed like the techno songs Ned liked, like birds, but I kept on kissing Ned. It went on for a while, I figured it was air hissing from the unicycle's tire. In front of me, I could see Ned's eyes, brown and almond shaped. Then the strangest thing happened. The room lit up with fireflies, hundreds of them — no, thousands — flying through the air and tickling my skin, stinging where the bruise swelled over my eye. After a second or so of their light show, they vanished. Poof. Like smoke.

"Mantis is dead, for sure," Ned said. He hugged me.

"Tell Grandpa thanks for the fireworks," I said. My bruise throbbed on my face, but I forgot the pain soon enough. Ned kissed me some more.

5

MADRE CATRINA

Pablo's wife, Eliza, casts a tagging device into the water, hoping she can track whatever's been living down in the shadows. They are seven miles west of the coast of La Poza Grande in Baja California. It is noon, but the water beneath them resembles tar. The water should be blue as sapphire out here. Instead, it's dark. It's so dark Pablo can see his reflection in the tranquil waves. Stubbly face, sun-dried leather cheeks, crinkled eyes, like his father's. Pablo and Eliza, emissaries of the biology department of Mexico's top university, both look like raisins.

It's their sixty-seventh day in a row in these waters, but Eliza has not given up. Pablo monitors their progress on his laptop. They have sat atop the oval-shaped dark spot for weeks, hoping to find its source.

There's a legend in the city of La Poza Grande that has inched its way through two centuries, digging its way under the sand in earthworm zigzags, passed down from family to family through stories. The men who heed the legend the most are the fishermen, because the rumor could be true. If it's a good legend, anyway. The best legends are the ones that have earned their grains of truth.

If you take your boat just a few miles out from La Poza Grande, where the wind caresses your cheek with a velvet touch and the sun warms the top of your head, they say you'll find a stain on the ocean. It's a shadow under the water, wider than ten houses and longer than a school bus. It is not the shadow of an ordinary whale, and if anyone knows how to spot a whale in the Pacific, it's the fishermen of La Poza Grande. Men who find the stain often genuflect and remove their boat from the area as fast as they can. It's said to be the ugliest monster of the waters, the devil's plaything.

They call the stain in the water Madre Catrina.

She earned this name when more than twenty fishermen disappeared in 1847 in a challenge to harpoon the giant whale that was said to be the source of the shadow. None of the fishermen came back from the trip. What did come back was Madre Catrina's name, playfully referential to Lady Death, the smiling, hat-tipped icon of Day of the Dead.

Pablo runs his finger along the water, wishing Eliza might actually take his advice and call the operation quits. The stress has worn her thin like gauze, and he feels her grow more distant every day, withdrawing into herself like a crab. She ties her hair in a ponytail now, and that always means he should brace himself, because she's about to impose solitude on him, whether he likes it or not.

Meals are their best time of the day, when they are no longer speaking the language of biology and migration patterns, when their working relationship ends and they have to start being themselves. He knows Eliza feels something strange for him. A certain kind of longing that extends beyond love, like a mutant limb that was never supposed to be there. Eliza understands his temper is more volatile than a rabid dog's, that he can't control his fits of anger, though of course, he never means to hurt her feelings. She tolerates his obsessions over money, his religious belief, the snowy dustings of his dandruff.

After they finish for the day, when he chews the broiled fish and sips his cold beer, he knows that the foundations of their marriage are like deer legs — beautiful, strong, but easily broken in two.

He's forgotten to turn on the marker but does so now, and his laptop begins to send signals immediately. There's activity, from below. Pinche Virgen Madre de Dios, he thinks.

Beneath, Madre Catrina stirs.

Eliza can see the Madre Catrina, too, and she screams to Pablo from the control room of the boat. It's too exciting to come out and see it with him in person. The numbers, dials and GPS shapes have her in a trance. This is one of the biggest moments of their lives.

The shadow that extends for hundreds of feet around their tiny boat shifts and undulates. The shape is as liquid as the Pacific currents, alive and independent. It changes then, as gaps appear in the darkness below, like tiny slivers of light peeking through the woods at dawn. Fat layers of shadow peel away, and it's clear within minutes that the onyx oval beneath them, Madre Catrina, is no monster of the deep.

Its parts are moving now, peeling away for a few moments in a slow dance. They rise to the surface and Pablo gasps when he sees the spouts of water splash around him like a battlefield.

Thick black skins burst through the water, slick as polished stone, each one a giant in its own right. Pablo's GPS shows there might be up to 250 whales under him right now. He worries they might tip the boat over, but he somehow doubts it. Madre Catrina does not have death in the cards for him, not today. She's got every Mexican accounted for, however. She'll come to collect him one day.

Pablo screams in joy. Data is pouring into his instruments, and joy is spilling from his mouth like a flood with each gush of laughter. He screams "I love you!" to

Eliza, and she sends him a message via the computer, *"Te quiero mucho."* It vanishes from his screen as the Madre Catrina whales fill the LCD with blips.

They are re-forming again, patching up the holes they made just minutes ago, becoming one giant organism dark as night, menacing as a whole, safe within the shadow they cast. They are immune to predators this way. They remain a family unit, making night their own, as an affront to daylight.

Eliza puts her hand on Pablo's shoulder, and he turns to look at the creases in her eyes, and how tightly the hair at her temples has been pulled back by the rubber band. The sun is in his face and he has a hard time seeing the details of her face, yet he knows the soft lips and the black eyes that smile under the weight of the noontime shadows. He knows her lips like a map. She could bear sons and daughters for him one day, though he's happy just listening to whales in the Pacific. That's all he needs.

Eliza looks so distant from him he could weep, yet the baritone tremors of the whales under his feet, and the shadow they cast upward, give him comfort and the promise of something off in the distance like a beacon. He supposes the whales beneath could eat him and his wife right now if they so chose, but that would be the stuff of legend. He asks Eliza to let her hair loose, and she frowns at him, relishing her silences. His laptop is making music, and the GPS avatars of Madre Catrina sing with a chirp every time the satellite finds them. Pablo relaxes his shoulders and listens to their breathing.

6

VICTORIA

Wednesday marked the end of a life for Victoria. It also marked the beginning of a new one.

Victoria's hair had fallen out in a few small patches in the back of her head over the years, starting roughly around the time she began her master's degree in microbiology at the University of Iowa. Twenty years had passed, and the patches were still there, like battle scars of her hard work. She was sure if she paid off her current debts, her chestnut hair might cover up its patches some day, coming back just as her own health would come back. She might even be able to wear her hair short someday.

She tucked her hair into her old White Sox baseball cap and stepped off the bus, which clanked and slogged as she walked a half block to the three-story greystone. The wooden door before her was shined to such a high polish she could see her own creased face in it as she turned the key and let herself in.

House No. 39, along Goethe Street, was the last family home Victoria would have to clean. She was fully matriculated at the university again, with a fat amount of savings in her bank account, and there was no turning back. She was going to finish her Ph.D., no question about it. Her dissertation sat on a digital file on her computer desktop back at home, and she would now have the freedom to finish it. No more filthy bathrooms, hand washing of cloth baby diapers, no more mopping.

She would never have to clean chum, either.

Inside, leather upholstery, furniture polish and the latest high-end gadgets greeted her in silence. She knew the last name of the family was Myer, but had never met any of them. Every time she let herself in, the palatial home rang hollow as a ghost house. Part of her agreement with the cleaning agency is that Victoria would only clean when there were no family members present.

After she made the beds, cleaned the three bathrooms and dusted, Victoria made her way to the stainless steel kitchen, which in itself was larger than her one-bedroom apartment. Next to the trash she found a red plastic bag with a biohazard symbol on it. She threw it over her shoulder and went to the back of the house.

She placed the bag in a plastic tub and removed a thick lump of grey/yellow matter. It smelled so bad she needed a surgical mask to tolerate it. She sprayed some of the chemicals the agency provided for her right on the grey lump and waited ten seconds while it sizzled. Kneading the mucous lump like a rising ball of bread dough, she used the strength in her shoulders to break it down from a solid mass into liquid. It gave off more noxious fumes like an angered skunk.

There were only two other chum cleaners in the city, catering to only the richest families. They each covered their own territory: Aida the North Shore suburbs, Teresa cleaned in Lincoln Park, and Victoria laid claim to the Gold Coast. Victoria's agency hadn't bothered to find her replacement. And she no longer cared. That would be her clients' problem.

After she was done with the chum, she went back in the house, where she put dishes away and soaked a set of plates in a special dish full of chlorinated disinfectant. The smell that comes off the plates plunged into her nose with notes of rotten fruit, ammonia and something worse. A slick bloody film clung to their rims. She scrubbed hard with a metal brush. Dishes used for eating man meat always had to be separate from those for regular foods. It was like keeping Kosher in post-war times. Nonetheless, the Myer family spent good money on nice white ceramic dishes for eating humans.

Human flesh was neither succulent

nor tender. For those types of carnivorous delicacies, one could go to Gibson's and order a steak, or visit west Randolph for hand-massaged Kobe beef, accentuated by a goblet of Cabernet. Human meat was simply utilitarian, an accidental miracle. Human meat, as it had turned out, was the fountain of youth.

Protein JLTC-19-47, extracted through a rigorous laboratory process during the Stem Cell Revolution of 2015, had proved to be an augmentation beyond breast milk: Both children and adults could benefit from the protein, boosting their immune systems and adding years to their lifespan. Scientists at Carnegie Melon had synthesized it over the period of two years, but it wasn't until 2073 that a large pharmaceutical company patented the process by which protein JLTC-19-47 could be extracted using a simple chemical solvent. The addition of chicken flavoring came about in 2075, and the name Ambrosevia was launched to the public.

The product's method remained grim as ever: To make the protein, one needed to place human flesh, internal organs included, in the solvent and eat the flesh, partially raw. It's essential that the meat be chewed raw; high temperatures destroyed the protein. Though scientists continued to attempt to synthesize the protein in a lab, flesh was the only way to access it.

And thus, Ambrosevia became the joy and luxury of the wealthy and the privileged. At first the vanity of rich women created a robust market. As the years went on, men began to enjoy the rejuvenating benefits of Ambrosevia. Who didn't want fewer grey hairs, more longevity, bigger muscle mass and more energy? To obtain the meat, one could enter into a contract with shipping companies, which delivered neatly wrapped bundles of meat to homes on a weekly basis.

That's where chum came in. The cooking process in the solvent left behind a soft grey mound of gristle (and sometimes tendon) that was both toxic and foul. Victoria's work in biology labs gave her the skills needed to dispose of chum properly and, thus, wealthy families could hire her services for a fee. The making of beds and kitchen bathrooms was almost incidental.

And here it was, her last house. She was no longer the perky-breasted singer of younger days. She wore her forty-three years well, and she took good care of her body but, inevitably, her sandpaper skin and arthritic joints only revealed the fact that she had been cleaning houses a very long time. She wished for fairness, for privilege even, but it was no matter. There was no changing the fact that she had got this far in life by helping human beings consume other human beings.

Victoria put the treated chum in a clean plastic container, neatly labeled for pickup. The smell remained suspended in the air for a few minutes like a ghost of rotted meat, sulfur and chlorine. She locked up the house and waited along LaSalle Street for the bus. Within a few minutes, the armored vehicle, loaded with more machine guns and rockets than a tank, appeared. She pressed her bus card against the reader and took a seat. She only had a few miles to travel back to her apartment in Rogers Park, but the eight miles between the Gold Coast and her home were treacherous.

Lincoln Park was the only neighborhood left between the Gold Coast and Rogers Park. After 2045, the razed and war-torn buildings had been converted into pristine green space, grass and tree-lined fields that no one could enjoy.

The packs of feral humans that took over the parks after the Chicago Reconciliation in 2050 would never give up their green parks. And they were not very tolerant of people like Victoria, who to them were privileged, with skin intact, two eyes and working organs. If it weren't for the electric fences, the whole city would belong to the feral packs.

Victoria began to doze as the bus made its way along a narrow valley of fenced-in pavement. It was only three in the afternoon, so the parks remained tranquil. The ferals only emerged when invaders strayed off the fenced-in border and, of course, at night.

Victoria would be home soon with her cat, Chiunes, and she could wash off the stink of chum from her fingers and think about putting in some time on her dissertation while listening to some old-time jazz. Within a year they would call her doctor. And she might be able to think of a better life for herself, away from the Rogers Park slums, in a home not infested by cockroaches, where she could look at Lake Michigan without UV glasses and afford UV coating on all her windows, like every decent person should.

Thank you, Ambrosevia. Thank you, chum.

After she locked the door behind her, Victoria smiled to herself. She could make a new life for herself, even at the age of forty-three. It was possible to begin anew. She felt certainty humming inside her heart. She rummaged in her fridge for ingredients for dinner that night, choosing the fresh scents of the lemons in the crisper. Hell, she might even pour herself a glass of wine tonight. She was about to change her life.

7

TINCTURE
DRK-01

Love Treasure came from a simple recipe, really.

To make the tincture, Lenoire put fish liver, dandelions, egg whites, pigeon feces, octopus ink and simple syrup in a steel bowl and stirred. She boiled the mixture over medium heat for ten hours and then diluted the reduction with filtered water and disinfected it with a few drops of rubbing alcohol. The runny black liquid was poured into artisan apothecary bottles and sold to those seeking to make someone fall in love with them. Laughable, definitely, but not to Lenoire. To her it meant steady business.

She set the last four of the ten bottles on display in a neat row next to the cash register. She made only ten units a year. The paper label on the brown glass advertised "Love Treasure, the potion to win them all." A novelty item, to be sure, but one of the shop's best sellers. Down in the basement, she kept a larger bottle, labeled DRK-01, with some reserves.

Of course, Lenoire's shop also sold handmade soaps and bath oils made by her husband, Ruben, her college sweetheart. They had opened up Green Bath Products in a shitty storefront next to a wig shop in Ukrainian Village on a whim in the mid Nineties, and their youthful whim had become, over the years, a business. She could hear Ruben in the lower level now, moving boxes around as they ran through spring inventory.

A short man, face like a chipmunk and arms thick like a construction worker's, came in through the door. His green eyes, ebullient and bright, lit up his face in a wide grin and clear brow. He hunched his shoulders as he browsed the hand moisturizers, the face scrubs, the tiny, nugget-sized loofahs. His neck craned as he looked for something in the aisles. No doubt, this man was uncomfortable in the shop, but he was in love. Lenoire could spot the lovesick immediately.

"Do you carry Love Treasure here?" the man asked.

Lenoire took one of the bottles from the display. "Love Treasure is meant to be used a couple of drops at a time," she said, "in a cocktail, or even as an aromatic in a bubble bath." It gave off an earthy

46

smell reminiscent of skin and cool moss. Women and gay men bought Love Treasure most often, but lately straight men came in for a bottle as well.

"My girlfriend sent me to find this stuff. She swears by it," he said with no trace of irony. "She's sent me 'cause she ran out of it."

"You both take Love Treasure, correct? It only works if you both take it," she said. Two winks danced in Lenoire's right eye.

"Funny," he said. "Hey, my girlfriend sent me to get this weird-smelling stuff, but who cares? It makes her happy, and I've never met a better lady. Ever. You ever been in love?"

"Of course. It's essential to living. Like air."

"You got it, lady. You know what I'm talking about then."

She scanned the bottle's bar code with the laser in her hand and eyed him over.

The man scratched his skin, right at the collarbone, where two red dots, not too dissimilar from acne blemishes, punctuated his skin above his brown chest hair.

"You got anything for this rash?" he said.

Of course, a love tincture such as the one Lenoire manufactured did not come without a price. The person who wanted to use the potion on their potential lover would experience dizziness and stomach pains for a week or so as a small egg sac, the size of a fig, grew in the back of their throat. If they successfully kissed their potential lover (and the fish liver and octopus ink made marvelous aphrodisiacs to make it so), the eggs, transparent and filmy like spittle, would transfer to the lover-to-be. Then, over the course of a few days, the eggs would germinate, allowing one single parasite to live in the stomach lining, eating the rest of the transparent eggs for nourishment. The parasite, which to be fair, was nothing more than a scorpion, would then burst through the stomach lining and move up the vertebrae (safely. of course, and without pain to the host), growing as it crawled.

By the fifth day, the scorpion would grow to full adulthood, about the size of a cat, and drape itself piggyback style over the host's shoulders, so the scorpion's pincers would cross over the heart, and the stinger would be situated immediately behind the rib cage, secreting a poisonous toxin at regular intervals.

Lenoire had considered naming the tincture Love Insurance when she first developed it. That name would have been accurate, but a marketing disaster.

"Sorry, you'll have to go to the drugstore for that rash," Lenoire said.

She put the tincture into a paper bag with his receipt. The man thanked her and turned his stocky frame toward the door.

Lenoire could see the odd angles of something sharp and slightly pointed between the man's shoulder blades, but as soon as he started walking, the illusion of movement was gone.

If the lover should think about falling out of love, the scorpion would release more toxin. If he or she should stray and cheat, the creature would squeeze its claws over the chest, ensuring fidelity through blinding pain. It was only when the original love host fell out of love that the scorpion would recede and dissolve into the flesh. Of course, the other way to get rid of it was to expose it to air, but that would mean surgery or murder, neither of which was very desirable or fashionable.

It was said the scorpion could kill its host if the original lover fell out of love, but in her thirty years in the business, Lenoire had never seen that happen.

From the basement, more noise and shuffling. Then steps. The door behind the cash register opened.

Ruben emerged from the stairs and rubbed his clean-shaven cheek all over her neck. He nuzzled Lenoire for what seemed like hours, though it only lasted a few minutes. "I am so smitten with you," he said. "Just like when we met in English lit 30 years ago. My Lenoire."

She kissed him, glad to have his touch, his company. She brushed aside thoughts of witchery, business plans and marketing strategies for the shop. It wasn't good to only think about work. Too much work and no play, *et cetera.*

She focused on Ruben. She held him close, and she rubbed the sharp lines of bony cartilage that poked out from the back of his white button-down, right under his neck, behind his rib cage. Through the front of Ruben's shirt, she felt his heat pressed onto her body. The two hornlike protrusions that crossed over his heart poked her for a moment, but she didn't mind. His mouth tasted sweet as snowflakes.

DIG YOUR OWN HOLE

Dirt tastes good, but Dad tells me not to eat it.

"Why?"

Because it can get you sick.

I lick my fingers and keep working. Too hot out here! My hands are too little for the spade. I want my own spade and bucket.

"Dad, how much longer? I'm hot. I'm thirsty."

Just a little more. You know your sister's baby bathtub? We need to make a hole that big.

It's getting dark already outside. Or maybe there are clouds? Dad says an eclipse is coming at three o'clock.

"Dad?"

Yes?

"When is three o'clock?"

Soon. Way too soon. Just keep digging, okay?

"Is it three yet?"

My dad snorts.

"But the dirt's hard and there are bits of rock. I'm getting tired."

I know, son. Not much you can do about that. These holes need to be finished by the time the eclipse begins. Gotta dig.

He makes a gesture like digging's supposed to be real fun, but it's not fair, I want to tell him. My hands are little, and his are big. He can stick the shovel in the dirt faster than me. I want to cry because I want to go back in the house and play, but I know I have to finish.

Dad puts the shovel aside and spits at the ground. I spit, too, just like him. He's strong.

Then he starts digging with his hands. He's got dirt on his white T-shirt and he's sweaty. He smells funny, too. His right hand looks just like mine. The other's not the same.

"Dad, what happened to your hand?"

Son, you asked me before. I told you, it happened a long time ago. Not important right now.

"I know, but what happened? Why don't you have all your fingers?"

He digs with his right hand, scooping out rocks and dirt. He looks funny. Like a chicken digging up dirt in a coop. Goofy Dad.

"Why isn't Mom out here?"

She dug hers yesterday. Do you ask her this many questions when it's the two of you and I'm at work?

"I don't know. Where's Mom?"

I told you, she's inside. Resting. Her eyes hurt.

"But she's blind, Dad."

I know, son. Even blind eyes can hurt. Today's a day for that. Looks like you're almost done.

The dirt inside the hole is cool, and it feels wet, like clay. I leave two handprints just like the ones we make at school sometimes. I look up at the clouds, and I can see the moon's getting close to the sun. It's not so dark. The real dark is different.

"Dad, did Mom ever tell you about the dogs and the cats?"

We can't get either one, son. Not yet.

He's not paying attention to me. He's poking his two fingers into the dirt. Then he takes a drink from a can with the other hand.

"No, Dad, the cats and dogs. I hear them in the walls."

Son, cats and dogs don't live in the walls.

"I do, I hear them all the time."

Son, that's the stuff of fairy tales. Everyone knows cats and dogs don't live in the walls. Didn't your mother explain to you it's just a story in a book?

"No."

The sky's getting darker, and the clouds are black and purple, like when it storms. The sun's still up there, but I look away. Dad says I should always look away from the sun or I'll end up like Mom. I can hear the house shaking. It does that sometimes. My dad doesn't turn around, but I think the dogs and the cats are back.

"Can you hear them? Dad, will the dogs and cats play with me?"

No, son. That's why we're digging. Always digging, so you won't imagine things like the dogs and the cats.

"Dad, why are we digging? My arms are tired."

So that the things that happened to me and your mother won't happen to you or your baby sister. It's for your own good.

I hear something boom from far away, like an elephant. It sounds big.

I don't want bad things to happen to you. The world's a tough place, Miguel. It's hard to stay safe. So you must listen to your parents.

I walk over to Dad's hole and I put my hands in the dirt. I am already finished with mine, and I want to help him get the dirt out. But then he pushes me back, hard, and I fall on the grass, and my back hurts. There's dirt all over my shirt, and I don't like when my shirts get dirty.

Son, stop crying.

"But you pushed me!"

I go back to my dad and try to help him dig again. This time he squeezes my arm real hard.

Son, no. And stop crying. If you want to survive this eclipse, and you want the Sun God to spare our house, you must do this right.

"Dad."

He doesn't care that I'm crying. He looks tired. I'm scared.

If you don't want the dogs and the cats inside the walls to come out, son, you must dig your own hole. This is how it works. I can't do it for you. Even your baby sister dug hers yesterday. Today it's our turn. The men.

"And Mom?"

I told you. She dug hers yesterday.

Finally, we finish, and my tears dry up on my face. My dad gets the dollies from inside the back porch and he hands me mine. It looks just like me, with the red shorts and white shirt. Black hair just like me, too. A smiley face. I put it in the hole in the ground and I start covering up. My dad's got a new can out and he's drinking from it.

"Dad, can I see your dolly?"

Yeah, hurry up before I cover it up.

I stand over it. Half of it's covered in dirt, all the way up to its belt. It's bigger than my dolly, that's for sure. And its right hand only has two fingers, just like Dad.

We put these in the ground, son, and the eclipse spares us. We're going to cut it close this decade. I should have started this much earlier this year, but, well.

"Dad, can fingers grow back?"

No, son. They don't grow back.

He pats the last bit of dirt on top of our dolls. Mommy's is next to mine. My dad says we have to go to church tomorrow after the eclipse, to be thankful.

Up in the sky, the clouds are now bright red and the sun and the moon are almost touching. I can hear the dogs and the cats in the wall now. He carries me in his arms into the house.

"Dad, do you hear them?"

Yes, son. I do. I think we're okay. The dogs and the cats, they're going to get louder, but if we did our job right, they'll pass right over us tonight. Even if they scream, or tear and scratch at the wood, you have to remember we did our jobs. Our voodoo dollies keep us safe, son.

The dark is creeping and I feel hot. The wind is blowing my hair, but it's hot wind, feels nasty. The house is making squeals, but I grab my dad's hand anyway as he takes me inside to the kitchen. When he closes the door I can hear the dogs and the cats crying inside the walls, screaming sometimes like little babies or like monsters. There's something scratching at the door cellar in the kitchen, but my dad just passes me the plate of mashed potatoes and keeps eating. My sister's in her chair, and Mom's smiling. It's not my bedtime yet.

Dad pours me a Coke while my mom gives me a plate of meatloaf. Meatloaf is my favorite.

9

LEMONADE:
AN ELECTRONIC
OPERA IN SIX PARTS

Playbill
Lemonade:
An Electronic Opera in Six Parts
Tezcatlipoca Opera House
Sky Stage, Cavern 77
June 30, Year 5-River
All Roles Sung by
10101010111110011101001010
and The Army of
111110101100100101010101111010
Composed by
Android 606-54-ZTKA
and
Erinye

Synopsis
ACT I

"Lemons up to the face!" scream the voices of a new nation. It is the year 20-Rabbit, and The Republic of Rain is celebrating its tenth anniversary. The

Seven-Headed Hydra, our narrator, emerges from the crowd as she devours men whole, and she begins to tell the tale of the Republic's bloody history. The crowd gathered at the civic square places lemon slices over their eyes while proclaiming President Lord Arboris as their national hero. The Hydra reveals her 3,000 eyes, grinds her shark teeth and begins the tale of how a nation was born.

ACT II

The Hydra's tale brings us back fifty years earlier. Arboris has been elected president of the nation of IXXXA for the third time. Outside the palace, a monsoon approaches, and the boisterous Arboris is celebrating the birth of his sixth son, Anubis. The infant is born in the midst of the storm, which destroys the national palace's sugar walls, killing those inside. Only two of Arboris' children survive: Zephyr, the oldest, and the newborn. Political tensions build as the inner states seek to secede themselves from the nation of IXXXA.

The royal infants' Gorgon nannies raise them for the next twelve years. When Zephyr is 18 and Anubis 15 years old, the Mechanized Angels of the Stoker Mountains raid the new national palace, and they kidnap Zephyr, leaving President Arboris with a single son, Anubis.

ACT III

Twenty years pass after the raid on the national palace, and Anubis has grown into a brooding and irritable adult. During a trip to the jungles, he meets a sacred printing press in the heart of the wilderness. Her name is Alixia. Through erotic machination and mecha-human fusion, he falls in love with the mystic Alixia. Mecha-human love is forbidden, and Arboris forbids his son from entering the jungles ever again. In a fit of demonic anger, Anubis enters the jungle one night and rapes and murders the printing press, disposing of her metal parts in a cave near the river. When Arboris learns of his son's brutal act, he banishes him from IXXXA for life.

ACT IV

Alone and anonymous, Anubis spends the next ten years wandering the planet, finally settling in the City of Numbers, a peaceful place that requires no country affiliation but exists unto itself, interlocking its towers and giant gears to the skies through a series of mathematical theorems.

Anubis still yearns for the love he discovered in Alixia the printing press, and one night, as he spirals upward through a rhomboid spire, he meets, Clara, a young human alchemy student, in the Museum of Iterative Mathematics. He falls deeply in love. Anubis expresses a joy and happiness that forces the beetle horns in his shoulders and the batwings at his back to sprout again, despite the clippings he received like every IXXXA child. He loves Clara, but he can also feel the silent urges of the Blood Luna, the ruling goddess of his people.

Clara takes Anubis straight into the center of the museum, and she invites him to bathe with her in the Lava Baths so he may be able to gaze at the mountains and oceans of the number Pi with her. Anubis sings a song of heartache and love when he sees the beauty of Pi, but upon the couple's mental return to the museum, Anubis is overcome with his savage urges. He throttles Clara to death, leaving her to swell into a blackened, bloated corpse. Anubis escapes the city as the police search for Clara's killer.

ACT V

In the Stoker Mountains, a pealing crack of thunder rips Mount Hikari in half, and from its peak rises Zephyr, who has spent two decades in the halls of the Mechanized Angels. The Angels have shown him the dark digital magic of the mountains. He emerges limb by limb, a giant made of human bone and cockroaches, as big as a castle and wholly an abomination. He flies away from the

Stoker Mountains on bronze wings in search of his brother, Anubis.

Anubis spends the next year alone, living in the swamps under the Metallurgy Woods, singing to the mushrooms that live away from the light. It is during this time that his blood thirst begins anew, and month after month, he murders those who cross his path and the females who fall in love with him. He develops a more refined taste for blood.

One night, after killing a dozen farmers in a Dionysian blood bath, Anubis swallows one of the farmer's sacks of sine-wave lemons. He chews and glows in the dusk. Anubis renames himself Lemonade. It is during his renaming ceremony in the swamp that the monstrous figure of Zephyr emerges from the silicone swamp. Zephyr curses Anubis for his own maladies, but Lemonade has almost forgotten who he once was. He can only taste his hunger on his tongue. The brothers battle, and Lemonade rips his brother's cockroach thorax with a single bite, emerging victorious. He places his brother's severed head on his own as a crown of victory.

ACT V

It is the eve of Arboris' fifth presidential term, and he is to inaugurate a nuclear park in his honor. Reports of a wave of serial killings in the country reach the capital, but no one has any solid details on the unknown murderer, who severs his victim's heads.

During the Dance of the Million Eagles, a presidential inauguration tradition, Arboris is pulled away by his advisers to his quarters. They say a visitor asks to speak with him right away. Lemonade awaits his father. When they meet, Arboris reels in disgust to learn of his son's bloody legacy. Lemonade has come back seeking redemption, but he receives none. As Lemonade cries his mercury tears, the chamber fills with liquid. The tears will not cease, and the liquid rises.

Arboris swims close and condemns his son to the Halls of Infinity. Lemonade, confused about his urges to kill and melancholy over his father's rejection, lunges at Arboris, biting his neck open in the process. When Arboris realizes he bleeds the same black blood as his son, he forgives him, but it is too late. His life escapes him in a fine geometrical vapor. He will die within a fortnight from his son's poisonous bite.

ACT VI

The following night, the final votes in the Spectral Senate are being counted, and the steam-powered spiders of the twelve Senators begin building the final tapestry to announce the election results, which will include the referendum on IXXA's changeover to a republic. Arboris, now aging and close to the lips of death, is seated next to his son.

As the spiders begin to announce the winner through a portrait they draw on the tapestry, Lemonade reveals to Arboris that he killed his brother, Zephyr, after he emerged as a monster from the mountains. Arboris' heart breaks, and thousands of black flies burst from his chest. No one can ever know of the murder, he tells his son. But Lemonade tells his father there is a better way to ensure silence. He swallows Arboris whole, knowing the presidency is always handed down to the next of kin.

Lemonade, the nation's most infamous killer, will rule as the president of the republic. Yet inside, he emits radio waves of mourning for a hundred years, alone, loveless and forever wandering the maze of his brittle digital heart.

10

A CONVERSATION WITH THE ELEPHANT

Rhinoceros ripped the audience to shreds at the last show of the last leg of the last tour they would ever perform. The show should have been historic, but the truth was, they did it for the cash, for the pussy and, mostly, to not be bored the fuck out of their minds by their shitty lives. They did it so they wouldn't slap the shit out of their children, the product of their mediocre marriages back in the shitty suburbs. The better days of Rhinoceros had passed, but they would use every bit of professionalism they had to blow the house down.

For one night, they were going to keep their dream alive. The Olympia was sold out.

Rhinoceros, most well known for their top-forty hit, "Asphyxia" back in the late

Nineties, had eventually been relegated to bargain bins and nostalgic pockets of drunken college memory. They did, however, have a single, effective trick up their sleeve at every show.

During the second encore, Rhin always played "Slowly for Those," a melancholy number that churned and pounded like the fury of a cyclone set to slow motion. While drummer Darren Garcia put the thumping snares into overdrive, the nauseating buzz saw of Rick Nuncio's guitar induced seizures in several concertgoers and caused pregnant women (and in some cases, those who didn't even know they were yet pregnant) to miscarry. Lead singer Cheetah tore through the lower depths of his range every single time he spat out "Slowly for Those."

Despite the harmony of light and the weight of the dark, balance and counterbalance, there was one single element that made "Slowly for Those" a rock monster of a song. It came from India's bass guitar from the very start of the chorus, but it built over eight minutes to an intolerable low rumble, like an airliner taking off inside each person's cranium. To hear that bass line was to hear the howls of the damned. India had named the infamous bass line "the Elephant" in a Rolling Stone interview, and years later he was still signing CDs not just as India, but as India, "Keeper of the Elephant."

Tonight, the first half of the show had been a showcase for the upbeat numbers, for the ones that got girls jiggling tits and frat boys swaying like sick cattle. The last half of the set, brooding and slow, always induced stupor in the crowd, but Rhinoceros didn't mind. A trance was better than a cup of beer in the face. Of course, right before the encores, they always closed the main set with the punker thumper, "Hail to the Chief," which Trent Reznor had once dubbed "a song worthy of christening the Anti-Christ to." The crowd slam danced, oblivious to its own beer bellies and sagging faces. But no matter what happened, "Slowly for Those" was always, always the last song.

10:15, Saturday night. They were almost done now. Only one thing left to do.

The four band members looked at each other the way brothers might before a game of baseball, and the first notes of "Slowly for Those" began their magic. The dance of Cheetah's raspy vocals, the pitter-patter of death from Garcia's high hat and the Nuncio distortion brought tears of blood to the men in the audience. The women felt stabbing needles in their nipples, but that didn't stop the audience from swaying in a single undulation as the song rolled out its waves of melancholy, hate and animals kept in cages for far too long.

It was unclear who felt the pain of the

song deepest in their core. Was it those who had lost lovers? Or was it those who sought to find other miserable souls to share meager moments of all-too-brief lives? Or was it perhaps the four members of Rhinoceros who felt their guts wrung like strings of rope over abrasive rock?

"Slowly for Those" pounded through the walls of the Olympia, and from the street, the venue drew stillness to itself, the way a street might quiet down before a car bomber rips it to shreds.

Five minutes into the iconic last song of the last set of Rhinoceros, India began the death march of his bass line, heading for the final crest of a career both banal and monumental. He forgot about his hemorrhoids and his whore of a mother, his credit card debt, and about how much pain he felt every time he saw his ex-wife. He forgot he was India, bassist for Rhinoceros.

The Elephant stepped into the Olympia.

The last three minutes of "Slowly for Those" did not overindulge. No jam sessions, no guitar solos, just the throbbing menace of a bass line that transcended India's fingers. Within three minutes, thirteen cardiac arrests, four strokes, nine cases of bloody diarrhea and 350 cases of spinal paralysis happened, not slowly and quietly, but instantly. Many would die, of course. About half of those who attended. But no one died in those three minutes of bliss. They all waited until after to do so. They needed to hear the Elephant. When the song ended, the applause died much too soon, because bodies had already collapsed onto the hardwood.

What happened that night in those last three minutes was difficult to ascertain. The song swelled beyond the mere scope of the speakers, and the light show faded as a purple light emanated from the backdrop, though its odd glimmer was not part of the show.

To this day, strange rumors of the last Rhinoceros set still float in the darker corners of the city and in the catacombs of the Internet. Many of the survivors report that the bass line of "Slowly for Those" spoke to each and every audience member as an elephant with black skin and white, milky eyes, a thing not of this Earth but of somewhere sinister, a place that had no business touching its edges to our own. And yet, for three minutes, everyone in Rhinoceros' grip was said to have glimpsed the creature's massive, bloody tusks and inhuman eyes that implied there was no end at the bottom of the spiral, only maddening smoke, eternal evil, endless concentric circles dancing in the notes of a rumbling bass guitar.

11

WE MERGE

We merge onto the left lane and the car squeals under us like a little girl on a rollercoaster. Before I can get my hands out in front of my face, we flip, over and over, like a toy, the woods and sky a kaleidoscope in the corners of my eyes.

It's six a.m., and it's my thirty-sixth birthday. It is not quite yet spring.

I look in the passenger seat and I check Nessa's pulse. She's alive and so am I. My heart beats slowly still, thirty beats per minute to be exact. Her shoulders slide under her at a forbidding angle, and thick blood cakes her lips. I place my hand on her forehead and press my consciousness onto her, for just a few seconds, before I breach her privacy. Then I pull away.

Our son is alive, perhaps shaken a bit. But he's alive. Nessa's legacy and mine, and that of the Third, will carry on. I bite my finger in order to make a blood sacrifice to the Dawn Behemoth for protecting my son. Thankfully, it's Nessa's third trimester, and the shell of the egg that sheaths him has extended protection to him. I slide my bloody thumbprint onto the glass and draw the rune to thank our Behemoth. If my son survives today, I will name my son after the king from the old stories of my youth. He will be Alacra.

I pull a hard shard of broken plastic from under my ass. Our GPS is broken into two ragged chunks. Circuit guts spill into the topsy-turvy.

When we squeeze through the window and onto the road, the sun blinds me for a moment. It feels good on my skin, like an old friend. Nessa is in blood, but it's no matter; it's a surface wound. My phone's time display shows that it's barely eight a.m. My wife's round belly brings me a crushing hug of comfort. She's more beautiful now than when we first met in an empty train car, each of us lonely, fractured, misunderstood.

Just as I am about to look for an emergency number, a bellow expands from the distance, where the two-lane blacktop vanishes in the distance. A tiny brown speck is moving toward us, like a truck. But the fuzzy speck moves much faster than any truck, and at jagged angles and in jumps that defy the laws of nature.

My worst fear is realized. The spider Dax has followed us from Houston. And now, without a vehicle, Nessa and I have no way to run but away from the thirty-foot monstrosity, hairy as a gorilla and with eight eyes smooth as pearls. I can feel recognition, but before I know it I have my wife's hand in mine, and we are running toward the black woods faster than we ever imagined our human legs could carry us. The spider's shadow is hard and black, much more so than the dark of the woods.

12

MACHINA

Home>App Store>Productivity>Machina

Machina
Category: Productivity
Released: October 3, 2015
Seller: LionDen Software, 2015
LionDen Software
5.0 MB
$0.99 BUY APP

APPLICATION DESCRIPTION

Meet Machina, the revolutionary app for the iPhone, iGlass, iMist and iPod Touch (versions 6.0 and 7.0), the portable version of the popular software package Deus Ex Machina. All the power of modern prophecy and dream interpretation are now available in the palm of your hand. Simply speak recollections of your dream into the device, and Machina will immediately capture the soul exhalations and spiritual nuances, processing your dream data within seconds. Machina is backward- and forward-compatible, allowing you to interpret dreams about the past and those that forecast events that are yet to come. Whenever Machina can gather enough detail, it renders a QuickTime version of your dream to watch and review. If you ever need to keep omens handy and accessible, you've found the right app.

FEATURES:

• Individual mappings of your dreams and where on the timeline of your life their prophecies materialize (99% accuracy).

• Customizable interfaces with multiple faith support: Christian, Judaic, Islamic, Buddhist, Wicca, Universalist, Pagan and non-denominational.

• Instant shareability of dream interpretation and prophecy through Facebook, Twitter and social media sites.

• A "Disperse" function to eject your omen into the spiritual ether (despite recent controversies over this feature, we have brought it back. You may disable in the preferences panel).

• A special adults-only mode for dreams of a sexual nature is available. (Parental controls available in Settings.)

• Full synchronization with iWork documents and Google Docs.

• Dream interpretations can be exported as spoken word, word processing documents or abstract photographs of the human dream brain.

• Languages: English, Spanish, French, Japanese, Aramaic, Hebrew, Chinese, Arabic, Greek.

Note: Machina does not support the interpretation of nightmares. The system will save recordings of nightmares but not process the data. Consult your physician if you are experiencing any difficulties breathing, loss of vision, paralysis or excessive bleeding. Machina is not supported inside places of worship; damage

73

may occur to your device if you run the app while inside a temple or church. LionDen is not responsible for broken equipment or data loss. Use at your own risk.

CUSTOMER REVIEWS
144 reviews
Write your own review

★★★

"I may as well sleep around for a while now — Machina said my dream of a human heart filled with worms means that I will find true love and marry during an international trip on the eve of my 27th birthday. With three years left to go, I know I can safely rely on one-night stands to satisfy my needs for now."

★

"I doubt this app works. I keep dreaming that the human race is collectively dreaming, building a city made of reeds and insect legs, like Tokyo if Cronenberg built it. The fucking app tells me there's some sort of Dream Collector coming to claim human consciousness in about 200 years. Looks like a cross between a buffalo and a circus freak. Hell if I know what that means. I just wanted to know if I was going to win the lottery since I dreamt about so much green, you know?"

★★★★★

"I have been dreaming of a maze made of mirrors for as far back as I can remember. I am 72 now, and it wasn't until I tried Machina that I realized that the maze is not leading toward the exit but farther into itself. As I've gotten older my agoraphobia has intensified, and in turn, the dream gets more intense. Toward the center of the labyrinth I hear the snorting and bellow of a Minotaur. Machina helped me understand the Minotaur will one day own me."

★★

"I fucking hate Windoze. APPLE4EVA"

★★★★

"Best app ever. I have dreamt of my grandmother's death a couple of times in the past month. Machina said it meant good things were coming, and it's true. Got a promotion and my wife told me she's pregnant. Just as predicted. Get this app now. Gramma's still kicking, too ;)"

★★★

"I keep dreaming my wife is cheating on me. It's so vivid that the line between waking and dreaming is fading. It's like, every time she goes out with her girlfriends she comes back drunk and with her clothes all wrinkled and makeup streaked and she gets in the bed and doesn't want to have anything to do with me. Oh wait."

★★★★

"LOL! Just Jailbreak your iPhone and run the hacked version of Machina. I let it interpret my nightmares, and they totally came true. I put in my bad dream last Christmas, and on New Year's some of my college buddies died in a house fire. Totally saw it foretold in the QuickTime clips in Machina. Go out and get it, peace of mind."

★★★

"I have dreamt so long about being a

75

Victorian aristocrat that I have made my own life in real time devoted to Victorian times. I wear the dresses, put on the wigs, even scrape my teeth with a stick. I've read every Jane Austen bio I can get my hands on. Yet, Machina told me my dream (in which I am Lady Edwards of Leeds), means only that I've been a carrier for vaginal warts since I was 19."

★★★★

"How the hell does the app know if I'm having a nightmare or not? I keep dreaming about the sunniest, nicest days, and it's exactly those dreams of blue skies that fill me with an inescapable dread, as if the ocean might rise in a deathly tidal wave or as if the sun itself might intensify its light and burn the planet to a glowing cinder. That " nice" dream of white clouds and blue skies is the most terrifying vision I have ever experienced in my life, and the app tells me it's a positive dream. All I can think about is how dread consumes me when I wake from the dream. Someone please help me."

<u>144 More Reviews</u>
Customers also bought
iExorcism
Metatron's 1000 Eyes
Pazuzu's Symphony
Ogami and Obake
Portable Hades
Lucifire
Black Curse
Witch's Sabbath
Amulet
Nephilim

AFTERWORD

Conflict is the driver of a good narrative, and whether a story is long or short, we are drawn to characters who endure challenges, to stories that take turns. During the summer of 2009, I was between novel manuscripts, biking along the lakefront in Chicago and turning over odd little story ideas over in my head. It was during one of those morning rides that I set out to generate a conflict for myself as a writer. I would write what I called micro fiction, short stories, limiting myself to a rough mark of thousand words. At the time I was working without an editor or a clear market for the stories. I simply knew I wanted to write varied narratives and write more than just a handful. I challenged myself to write a new story in a twenty-four-hour cycle. One story a day, for twelve days. That was the genesis of *The 12 Burning Wheels*.

As a writer I don't generally outline or plan very much in advance, though in this instance I did sketch some story titles for me to prime the pump. As I wrote each day, working with a limited amount of writing time and a single title to start from, I found that the narratives came to me and onto the keyboard without too much agony. Deadlines work, kids. At least for me, they do. The end result were stories that cut across setting and time, genre and style. "The Broken Chest" is probably the most conventional, telling a short tale of family relationships between father and daughter. "The Scryer," as is evident in several of the stories, hints at a larger narrative, and I imagine I might visit its gritty urban setting of Chicago and its world of magic shops and tools. Sadly, the narrator of that story doesn't stick around for long, but the world of Worm Queens is worth exploring in the future.

Music plays a big part not just in my stories, but also in the writing process itself. If you listen to Goldfrapp's "Deep Honey" and read my story "Honey" you'll see the connections I draw from what I hear in the music and in turn, connect to the mood of the story. "Honey," is the Circe myth retold from the witch's point of view and it's oh, so so sweet. "Mantis Love" is my one explicitly gay story, and it speaks to experiences of teens being out of the closet in high school, an experience I didn't have, but one which I have a lot of respect for. The whales of "Madre Catrina" still haunt me, though the story centers much more around the fractured relationship of the husband-wife team out in the dark Pacific waters. Often we ourselves are more frightening than the spectres of a narrative.

"Victoria" came in right in the middle. Its title came first. The story was originally called "Victoria the Cleaner" as a very oblique reference to the character Victor "The Cleaner" in the French film "La Femme Nikita". Yet, the story turned out to hold no assassins in it, no sleek handguns, no mini skirts.

"Tincture DRK-01" amuses me to no end. I had always wanted to write a story about a love potion.

"Dig Your Own Hole" is the story that unsettled me the most, and though the title did come from the Chemical Brothers' song, there's no other connection there. However, maybe the animal sounds in the walls could be awfully similar to their raucous breakbeats...

"Lemonade, An Electronic Opera in Six Parts" is part of a possible larger work. Part theater of the absurd and part opera, the tragedy of these two brothers feels real to me. In the story we only read through the synopsis in the program, but maybe I'll have to write one day about the experience of seeing the actual opera. I won't mind going back to this world of digital agents that compose operas.

"A Conversation with the Elephant," at its core, is the sound of the bass, and there you have it, I am back to talking about music again. There are many songs that have the sound of the Elephant, but in this case it's worthless to say which one inspired it. The reader is better off conjuring that song for him or herself.

"We Merge" is part of a future larger work, and rest assured, we will know much more about this strange couple and the reasons why Dax the spider hunts them.

And finally we have "Machina," done in the format of an iPhone app screen in the iTunes store. Download it now.

As a short acknowledgement, I'd like to thank my editors Kim Okabe and Chris Fletcher for working with my texts and helping them become better.

Though I generally write in longer novel form, I haven't enjoyed myself as much recently as I did writing *The 12 Burning Wheels*. Scryers, angry Greek witches, and feral humans in a future version of a dystopian Chicago – they unfolded before me over twelve days. Each day was a surprise. I thank you for taking time to read these stories and hope you enjoy them.

Cesar Torres
Chicago
December 2009

5209522R0

Made in the USA
Lexington, KY
15 April 2010